THE SPELLING BEE BEFORE RECESS

By
Deborah Lee Rose

Illustrated by
Carey F. Armstrong-Ellis

Abrams Books for Young Readers
New York

THERE IS NO "I"
IN TEAM

'Twas right before recess
(about 10:23).

Not a teacher was teaching
(not even PE).

The students were squirming,
but none made a sound,
as the spelling bee entered
its championship round.

LIBRARIAN

PRINCIPAL

From the whole school of spellers,
we were down to just three:
Cornelius ("The Genius"),
smart Ruby, and *me*.

Cornelius knew times tables
up, down, and through.
He knew all the state capitals—
presidents too.

Ruby played trumpet.
She lived right next door.
She'd read at least ten zillion books,
maybe more.

Kids called me "The Slugger."
I never struck out.
I memorized word lists.
I'd win this—
NO doubt.

The first words were easy, like

cupcake

and

spoon.

Turtle
and
sandwich
and
brain
and
balloon.

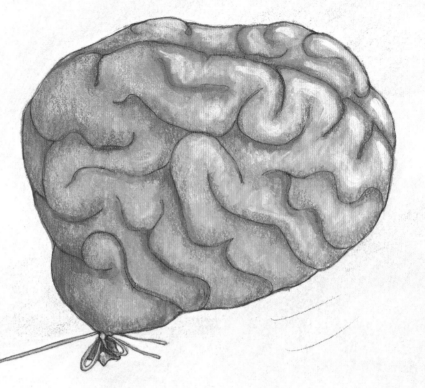

The next ones were harder.
The words seemed to **zing!**
I clenched both my fists,
and I took my best swing.

Cornelius got out
when he misspelled
mysterious.

MISTERIOUS

That left Ruby and me.
Things were getting more serious.

We spelled
reindeer
and
rumpus

and
llama
and
laugh.

Echo
and
gecko
and
ghost
and
giraffe.

The sweat from my armpits
was starting to show,
while Ruby looked cooler
than new-fallen snow.

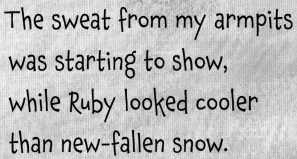

Back and forth,
forth and back,
we spelled
penguin
and
ocean.

Icicle,
bicycle,
mischief,
and
motion.

The words flew like fastballs
right over home plate.

Author.
Umbrella.
Pollution.
Equate.

Word after word—
we were in the ninth inning.
One minute to recess,
and **NO ONE WAS WINNING.**

"We're stuck at an impasse!" the principal said.
"So I'm going to try something different instead.
For the next word,
you'll spell *and* tell what the word means."

I groaned. All I'd memorized wasn't worth beans . . .

"SESQUIPEDALIAN," the principal uttered.

"That's not on the spelling lists!" several kids muttered.

I looked over at Ruby,
who nodded her head.
That's when I knew
I had something to dread.

Now the kids were all perched
on the edge of their seats.
It was my turn at bat.
I dug in my cleats.

"SESQUIPEDALIAN.
That's S— E— S— Q,
U— I— P— E..."
(I was more than half through!)

"D— and an A—
and an L— I— E— N..."

"Not quite," said Principal Wordsworth.
"Ruby, your turn again."

I was out! I'd been benched!
I felt like a jerk.
Ruby rose from her chair
and went straight to her work.

Her letters just floated,
like notes in a song . . .
By the end, she had gotten
NOT ONE OF THEM WRONG.

"Now, Ruby, please tell us,
just what does that mean?"

"It means someone who **USES BIG WORDS!**"

I turned green.

Like a batter who hears the ump's cry of
"Strike three!"
I slumped in my chair,
hoping no one would see.

Ms. Wordsworth was beaming.

"Our new spelling pro . . .
is Ruby Melgoza!" she said.
"Way to go!

To the top of the school—maybe even the state.
Ruby's shown us the meaning of how to be great!"

The recess bell clanged,
and kids sprang for the door.
I dragged my feet gloomily
over the floor.

Then I heard the librarian calling my name.
I knew she liked baseball—

"Hey, Slugger. Great game!"

"But I lost, Mrs. Booker. Didn't anyone
tell you?"

"So you lost—but not just because someone out-spelled you.

What Ruby knows best
isn't just how to spell.
She knows that what matters is to
use your words well.

So in spelling (and life),
if you want to succeed,
the best thing of all you can do
is to **READ.**"

As I ran to the playground
I felt nothing to fear,
till I heard her yell after,

"There's always **NEXT** year!"

SPELLING WORDS
PRINCIPAL WORDSWORTH'S LIST

author	reindeer	brain
ocean	balloon	sesquipedalian
llama	laugh	mysterious
sandwich	echo	rumpus
umbrella	ghost	gecko
penguin	icicle	spoon
bicycle	mischief	
motion	cupcake	
equate	pollution	
giraffe	turtle	

MORE WORDS FROM THE STORY

baseball	succeed	recess
students	their	shown
memorize	principal	librarian
doubt	floated	heard
presidents	capitals	misspelled
again	minute	great
squirming	someone	playground
easy	zillion	through
meaning	teacher	year
trumpet	after	state

For smart Ruby and smart Miranda, both readers extraordinaire.
And special thanks to Tom Chapin, who taught me a great big word
I didn't know. —**D. L. R.**

To my mom, who passed along an abhorrence of bad spelling and the
use of bad grammar by people who should know better . . . And yes,
I had to look up the spelling of 'abhorrence.' —**C. F. A.-E.**

The pictures were done on 90 lb. Arches hot press watercolor paper.
The figures were first outlined in ink, and then gouache was added
for a base of color. The shading and detail were achieved with layers
of Prismacolor colored pencil over the gouache.

AUTHOR'S NOTE

To create this book, I looked at hundreds of spelling words in lists
from public and private schools across the country. I chose words from
many school subjects and themes, including animals, language arts,
the environment, science, and math, as well as words that allude to
everyday kid stuff. I also chose words with lots of varied sounds and
letter combinations, and rhyming words with different spellings, so this
book is a lesson on many levels!

"Sesquipedalian" became the tiebreaker because Tom Chapin
uses it in his wonderful song "Great Big Words," and it's a word that
helped clinch victory for a real-life national spelling bee champ. Plus
the misspelling of it in the story includes the word "alien," which kids
probably do know how to spell! The fact that it means "inclined to use
big words" was perfect, and being able to teach its meaning along
with the spelling was so much fun.

To this day, I remember my own elementary school bee when I
spelled "similar" as though it rhymed with "familiar," and thus began
my love affair with the dictionary.

Publisher's Note: The spelling lists in this book—two on the previous
spread and one on the endpapers—may be used without requesting
permission. However, to use the story text or images you must obtain
the permission of the publisher.

Cataloging-in-Publication Data has been applied for
and may be obtained from the Library of Congress.
ISBN: 978-1-4197-0847-3

Text copyright © 2013 Deborah Lee Rose
Illustrations copyright © 2013 Carey F. Armstrong-Ellis
Book design by Maria T. Middleton

Published in 2013 by Abrams Books for Young Readers, an imprint
of ABRAMS. All rights reserved. No portion of this book may be
reproduced, stored in a retrieval system, or transmitted in any form
or by any means, mechanical, electronic, photocopying, recording, or
otherwise, without written permission from the publisher.

Printed and bound in China
10 9 8 7 6 5 4 3 2

Abrams Books for Young Readers are available at special discounts
when purchased in quantity for premiums and promotions as well as
fundraising or educational use. Special editions can also be created
to specification. For details, contact specialsales@abramsbooks.com
or the address below.

ABRAMS
THE ART OF BOOKS SINCE 1949
115 West 18th Street
New York, NY 10011
www.abramsbooks.com